Dragons, Phantoms, & Secrets

THE BEST NEW FANTASY FROM ARROW WRITERS

No part of this publication
may be reproduced, stored
in a retrieval system, or
transmitted in any form or
by any means, electronic,
mechanical, photocopying,
recording, or otherwise,
without written permission of
the publisher. For information
regarding permission, write
to Scholastic Inc., Attention:
Permissions Department, 557
Broadway, New York, NY 10012.

ISBN 0-439-74432-6

Copyright © 2005 by Scholastic Inc.

All rights reserved. Published by Scholastic
Inc. SCHOLASTIC and associated logos are
trademarks and/or registered trademarks of
Scholastic Inc.

12 11 10 9 8 7 6 5 4 3 2 1   5 6 7 8 9 10/0

Printed in the U.S.A.
First printing, June 2005

DraGons,
PHantoms,
& seCRets

THE BEST NEW FANTASY FROM ARROW WRITERS

SCHOLASTIC INC.

New York   Toronto   London   Auckland   Sydney
Mexico City   New Delhi   Hong Kong   Buenos Aires

CONTENTS ★★

PREFACE

Dear Readers and Writers,

In your hands, you hold a magical collection. The ten winners of the Arrow Fantasy Writing Contest have invented new creatures, new worlds, and even new words. But most of all, they have succeeded in doing one very important thing: writing a good story.

For years, I was an illustrator of other people's stories. After a while, I realized I wanted to create and illustrate my own stories. It didn't take very long for me to discover that I loved storytelling more than anything else I'd ever tried. And then I got lost in the magical world of writing fantasy.

When you write any story — but especially a fantasy story — it is important to let yourself get lost. Let yourself be transported to strange places. Invent new objects. Let magic swirl around and surprise you. But most importantly, listen. Listen to your imagination — and listen to your heart.

Enjoy the stories in this book. Then go and write your own!

Your fellow fantasy author,
Cornelia Funke

Cornelia Funke was born in Dorsten, Westphalia. She graduated from the University of Hamburg in Germany, where she received a degree in education theory. She then completed a course in book illustration at Hamburg State College of Design. Following that, she worked as a designer of board games and as an illustrator of children's books, which inspired her to become an author herself.

She has written more than 40 books, including the highly acclaimed *Dragon Rider*, *Inkheart*, and Wild Chicks series, and her books have been translated and sold in many countries. *The Thief Lord* has won the Swiss Youth Literature Award, the Zurich Children's Book Award, and the Book Award from the Venice House of Literature. After its American release, it also received the Mildred L. Batchelder Award for the best translated children's book of the year and several other accolades.

Cornelia Funke lives near Hamburg, Germany, with her husband Rolf, her daughter, Anna, and her son, Ben.

AUTHOR JUDgES

Jenny Nimmo was born in Windsor, England. Her love of books was evident at an early age. At nine years old she had already read all the books in her school junior library and begged for permission to join the senior library. Jenny realized early in her childhood that writing stories could be as much fun as reading them. So her years of writing and thrilling her friends with creepy stories began.

Her first award-winning book was *The Snow Spider* published in 1986. It was an instant hit and became the winner of the Smarties Grand Prix. It was later turned into a television children's fantasy drama in England. Nimmo's book, *Midnight for Charlie Bone*, is the tale of a young boy who has a newly found gift of hearing people talking in photographs.

Nimmo conducts a simple life of writing. She lives in an old watermill in Wales and begins her day of writing only after the chickens, rabbits, and cats have all been fed! During the summer she puts down her pencil to help her husband run a children's summer school at their home.

Since 1991, **Suzanne Collins** has had a successful and prolific career writing for children's television. She has worked on the staffs of several Nickelodeon shows. Most recently she was the Head Writer for Scholastic Entertainment's Clifford's Puppy Days, which premiered in September 2003.

Excited by the possibilities of a more literary form, she felt a strong urge to explore bringing characters and ideas to life in books. Thinking one day about *Alice in Wonderland*, she was struck by how pastoral the setting must seem to kids who, like her own, lived in urban surroundings. In New York City, you're much more likely to fall down a manhole than a rabbit hole and, if you do, you're not going to find a tea party. What might you find...? Well, that's the story of *Gregor the Overlander*, the first in a five-part fantasy series entitled The Underland Chronicles.

Suzanne Collins lives in New York City with her family.

AUTHOR JUDgES

Holly Black is the author of the best-selling series, The Spiderwick Chronicles, which has been translated into 27 languages worldwide.

Holly was born in a decrepit Victorian house in New Jersey. Her mother, a painter and dollmaker, fed her books on ghosts and fairies that formed much of her later views on the world. She is the also the author of *Tithe: A Modern Faerie Tale*, which was one of the ALA's Best Books for Young Adults and the New York Public Library's "Best 2002 Books for the Teenage."

Today, Holly lives in Amherst, Massachusetts, with her husband, Theo, and their many animals. She is an avid collector of rare folklore volumes and freaky furniture, spooky dolls, and crazy hats.

★ The Phantom Zone ★

By Christopher Armstrong

I pushed open the door of my laboratory. I stepped inside and felt for the light switch. I grasped it in my cold, clammy hand and turned on the dim, bare lightbulb hanging from the ceiling. I opened the refrigerator door and pulled out a container, left there 24 hours ago. Now, it was bubbling and turning a nasty shade of blue. It was designed to bring the dead back to life. I carefully picked up the beaker and set it in a machine in the center of the room. It fizzed and started to burn! Before I could stop it, a hole formed in mid-air!

I peered through and gasped, trying to hold back a scream. There was a glowing face staring at me! My limbs were frozen. A thin layer of glowing green ice covered my skin! I pulled myself backwards, but instead I floated toward the hole in the air. The face curled into an ugly grin and laughed a hideous laugh. My lips formed the word "NO" but no sound came out. I was pulled through the hole, almost as if I were one with the wind.

In fact, there was no air at all! I dropped limply, but strangely enough, I just kept falling. I was quickly running out of air, when I realized I no longer needed it. I was in the depth of space. I supported myself in the air and stared around. The hideous creature that brought me from Earth had vanished.

Suddenly a wind sprang up and lightning forked through the black sky. The wind spun faster and faster until a raging tornado formed. Shadowy phantoms formed and whirled around me. "It's an Earthling," they shrieked! As they drew closer, I held out my hand. Waves of blue light flew out of my hand and the fiend screamed in rage. The one that had brought me here screeched, "You will regret the wrath of the phantom zone. We have imprisoned you in the everlasting whirlwind. There is no hope!" I let off another blast of blue light! It shattered the wall of the tornado, but it reformed immediately. "So," exclaimed the phantom, who appeared to be the leader, "you have discovered the Earthling power. Your waves of light are useless against me."

In my mind, I had a plan. I targeted the space right below him. I fired light waves, which streaked across the black sky. I hoped that my sense of direction was correct. A hole formed and the phantom cried out. He was being sucked out of the tornado! The phantom had been so busy gloating he hadn't counted on my sense of gravity. The other phantoms shrieked and disappeared in a fiery holocaust of smoke and flame! The fires soon died down along with the whirling winds. I was free to go! I floated toward the hole in the sky. I had decided something. No more experiments, no more labs. Then I will be truly free!

What the Judges Said About
The Phantom Zone

"A story full of action and energy. Quite a difficult feat, well achieved."

About the Author
Christopher Armstrong

Christopher, a nine-year-old fourth grade student who lives in Connecticut, likes to read, swim, and listen to books on tape. He has a younger sister. Kaya, his white boxer, is also a 'member' of the family. Christopher would like to be a writer or a teacher when he gets older. His favorite part of writing a story is adding interesting and unexpected twists so it doesn't have to end quickly. His favorite fantasy author is J.K. Rowling. If he could be any character in a fantasy story he would be Eragon (*Eragon*) because he could ride dragons and meet cool people who live in castles.

The Angels of Cranwood
By Rachel Berzon-Fink

"Hello?" I whispered. "Who's out there?" I was all alone. How I wished one of my fellow Girl Scouts would find me. It was dark and there were so many unfamiliar noises. Then I heard it again. A quiet shuffling. Like someone walking on dead leaves.

But it was summer. There were no falling leaves. I made a run for it but I fell in a hole, full of mud.

I tried to pull myself out, but I was stuck, until someone yanked me out. "Thank you," I cried, but whoever it was didn't answer. The person was still there; I could feel his warm breath on my forehead.

Then it lifted me off the ground. It was like he/she/it had its hands on my shoulders and was floating! I stayed cradled in no-name's arms until the 'ride' was over. We landed on some kind of cave.

I was led inside. We sat down at a long table. My mouth was watering at the sight of ham; chicken; duck; steak; corn; potatoes; shrimp; and pasta.

It was getting light outside. I could now see this strange thing. He had saved me twice, but then scared me and kidnapped me. He was wearing a white cloak with a hood pulled tightly over his head, a huge nose, no teeth, and weirdest of all, he had WINGS!!!!!!

"Eat," he shouted in a low-pitched voice.

"Wh-wh-who are you?" I stammered.

"One more word," he bellowed, "and you will never see the light of day again."

"Sorry," I peeped. He calmly stood up. I ran and was almost to the entrance when about ten of this same person circled me. "Please spare me," I cried. One of the guy's arms flew off and pulled off another guy's head. He threw it at me.

I must have fainted from the blow because I woke up on an altar. The guy with the funny voice had turned himself invisible and had now appeared again. I cried, "You have no reason to hurt me."

All of a sudden a metal spear flew through the air and blasted him to the wall, but he remained alive and breathing. "You are safe now," said a calm voice. He had wings as well.

This new person was named Ivan. We walked back to my Girl Scout camp in Cranwood. As we walked, I noticed his feathers were falling one by one. When we saw the entrance, he sat down. "You know your way from here."

"What about you?" I asked.

"I'm not one to be near people."

So I left him. I was underneath the sign, about to go in, but I wanted to say thank you. I turned to wave, but now he was lying, stretched out, with his wings wrapped around him. I ran to him thinking he was hurt. But as soon as I took a step closer, he was gone. The only thing left were two golden feathers and, of course, my memories.

What the Judges Said About
The Angels of Cranwood

"The writer made an interesting choice of having a main character caught up in a battle she is far too weak to compete in."

About the Author
Rachel Berzon-Fink

Eleven-year-old Rachel lives with her parents and two Siamese cats, named Teddy and Oliver, in New Jersey. Rachel enjoys playing the cello, snowboarding, ice skating, cooking, and baking. She would like to be a chef, but does enjoy writing in school and making up stories in her head. Her favorite part of writing a story is the "middle." The middle is when all of the ideas swarm together and the story starts changing from what you've imagined to something even better.

★ Spirals ★★

By Sarah Borwick

She knew what she had to do. The spiderwebs around the entrance were whispering in the wind. The tunnel went straight down, spiraling, curling, twisting into the bottomless mist. She dove into the black hole. Suddenly, she was riding an ice cold waterfall, upside down, right side up, slow, fast, twisting, straight. She plopped onto a platform made of trees bent over, pillows covering it, so when she landed, the trees felt the movement, swung up, and bounced her into the air. Mist was everywhere.

When she landed, a strange creature greeted her, and called her a name: Spiral. Ahead of her was a jungle with a tree stump in front, and on that stump was a piece of paper and something sparkling. Spiral walked toward the stump, and as she grasped the paper and the sparkling thing that turned out to be rubies, the ground broke away, carrying Spiral and her things down a dark tunnel once again. In ten seconds she was very hot, the sun was shining very brightly. She read the faded paper:

You are in the world named after you. These are the jewels you need to find the hidden cave. Once in the cave, battle a dragon to reach more jewels so you may get back into your world. Find a piece of paper with the language of the strange creature that talked to you earlier. Go further through the cave to find my home. Give me the language to save our city from a curse.

Sincerely,
Spiralonoca
Leader of the Spirals' city

Wow, how was Spiral supposed to find a hidden cave? Maybe one of the three large rubies could be a map. She looked at the rubies in her hand. One had understandable writing on it. It said, "Hot, Cold." The "Hot" was circled and there was an arrow pointing ahead. "Great," she thought, "a childish game of hide-the object!" She stepped forward. A flame sprouted up from the ground. "Maybe not so childish!" she squealed. She carefully jumped over the fire. She saw a beautiful river and a long vine. Across the river was a big rock. She took a deep breath, grabbed the vine, pushed off the ground, and "Wheee," was suddenly at the other side. But Spiral was too scared to jump off. She swung there, back and forth, her hands slowly slipping off the rope; she couldn't stay on.

She fell into the river with a big splash. It was icy cold. The current was pulling her. She pulled her whole body and waded to the other side. She pulled a vine, which moved the rock and revealed the cave. It looked like there was a blazing fire around the corner. She guessed it was the dragon. Spiral reached into her pocket to get her pocket knife, but instead found a sword. She ventured around the corner. Spiral knew what she had to do.

She closed her journal and decided to finish writing her memoirs another day.

What the Judges Said About Spirals

"This has a fun device of pulling the reader into what they believe is a fantastical world, and then letting them discover that that world exists in a girl's head."

About the Author Sarah Borwick

Sarah is from Massachusetts where she is a student in the fourth grade. She has an older brother and stepsister and her family likes to play board games like Scrabble and Monopoly. Her favorite part of writing a story is thinking about what's happening next. J.R.R. Tolkien is her favorite fantasy author and if she could be any character in a fantasy story, it would be Bilbo Baggins from *The Hobbit*.

Hotdogzilla
By Juan Chapa

In a lab in Tokyo, there were two inventors working on a microwave that would prepare food in seconds. They were putting on the finishing touches and then, they finished. They made it so the microwave would be powered by radioactive waste. They needed something to test the microwave. "What should we use to test the microwave?" one of the inventors asked. "I don't know," the other one shrugged. He put his hands in his pocket and felt something. He pulled the object out of his pocket. It was a raw hotdog covered in hairs. "Will this do?" he asked, holding up the hotdog. "Yeah, that'll do," the other inventor said. So they popped the hotdog in the microwave. But something went wrong.

The microwave leaked its radioactive waste and covered the hotdog. The inventors immediately shut down the microwave. After that, they got a pair of tweezers and a jar. They carefully grabbed the hotdog with the tweezers and put it in the jar. Then, they put the jar in a refrigerator in the mess hall. The hotdog was not to be known of.

Years passed. The hotdog stayed in its preserved state. New people started working in the laboratory after it became a biology lab. The hotdog was still in the fridge until one night. One of the wolverines escaped. It went into the mess hall. It noticed the fridge and pulled on the handle. Finally, the fridge opened. The wolverine squirmed into the fridge, knocking aside some soda bottles until it came to the jar with the hotdog in it. The wolverine shoved it onto the floor and shattered the jar. One of the security guards heard the crash and ran to the scene. When he got there he witnessed the wolverine devouring the hotdog. Then, the wolverine started growing. The more it grew, the smaller and less visible its hair and tail became. It kept growing until it was a 100-foot-tall hotdog with wolverine features. The giant hotdog-like thing swallowed up the security guard and went off to destroy Tokyo.

When the hotdog (or Hotdogzilla, as people called it) got to downtown Tokyo, it made complete chaos. It munched up buildings, people, and other stuff. The Japanese military discussed a plan to get rid of Hotdogzilla. They decided to make a giant dart to suck up all the radioactive waste in him. "But sir," one of the soldiers asked another, "how do you know if Hotdogzilla has radioactive waste in him?" "Remember when Godzilla attacked Japan, bub?" another replied. So they loaded a giant dart onto one of the planes and made it take off. Soon enough, the giant dart was on Hotdogzilla. But it didn't work. Hotdogzilla just tore it out and threw it on the ground. Then a hobo noticed Hotdogzilla. He started nibbling on Hotdogzilla. Soon enough, there was nothing left of Hotdogzilla. Tokyo was saved.

What the Judges Said About Hotdogzilla

"*Hotdogzilla* stood out not only because it uses elements of classic science fiction, but because the writer has a good sense of humor as well. I love, for instance, that one of the scientists just HAPPENS to have a raw hotdog in his pocket. And that, without much worrying about the consequences, they stick the radioactive hotdog in the fridge for...you know...somebody else to deal with."

About the Author Juan Chapa

Ten-year-old Juan is from Indiana. He is the oldest child in his family and likes to snowboard, read, and play video games. Juan's favorite part of writing a story is using his imagination to create the story. His favorite fantasy author is Dav Pilkey, and if a fantasy character could be his best friend, Juan would choose Harold from *Captain Underpants*.

★Terror of Jungletonia★
By Monica Chen

Ordinarily, Janafoo enjoyed fishing on Tuesdays but foul weather was coming. After deciding he would hunt for small rodents, he sought permission from Juju, his tribal leader. Juju was washing at the sacred spring when Janafoo approached him.

"Why are you here?" Juju admonished Janafoo. Only tribal kings were at this spring.

Before he could reply, Juju's nephew dashed toward both monkeys. Mofo was a bloody sight with thick patches of fur missing.

"Mofo, what has happened? Is your father okay?"

Mofo said, "Ono'o has destroyed our village. No one is left but me." Juju and Janafoo gasped.

"Janafoo! Take my nephew to the healing monkey immediately. Tell all monkeys there will be a gathering tonight!"

Ono'o was the terror of Planet Jungletonia. He had battle scars adorning his face. Ono'o's only purpose was to kill. Juju came from a dynasty that ruled the monkeys for 500 years with fairness. He desired what was good for his people. Maybe Juju could ask the community to build a trap for the tiger at the meeting tonight. The wooden whistle cried out, announcing the meeting.

"Today," Juju began, "we gather to discuss one who dangerously approaches our village. This creature is..." Juju paused, "the terror of Jungletonia, the dreaded Ono'o." A gasp came from the monkeys. Juju continued, "But I have created a plan to trick him."

When the "voting" was done, Juju's assistant approached him. "Chief Juju, one monkey was not present: Salga."

Everyone knew Salga desired to be chief, but his dream was shattered by Juju. Juju thought, *perhaps Salga has set out to kill the tiger so he can be chief!*

"Don't worry about Salga. Please gather monkeys to begin building the trap."

Reaching Salga's hut, Juju knocked on the door. No answer. Stealthily, he stepped inside. Juju spotted a piece of bark with writing. To his horror, they were plans to assassinate Juju himself. Juju stalked out to hunt Salga down.

In the lush jungle, he saw something that made him stop. It was Salga. He was dead. The tracks around the carcass confirmed the worst. Ono'o was near.

The next day Juju leaned against a banana tree when he heard a vicious snarl. Ono'o glared at him and sprang. Juju aimed at the tiger but Ono'o cut a wound down the monkey's leg. Juju scampered up a tree, tore a banana off and pelted it at Ono'o. When the fruit hit the tiger, Juju leapt and landed on the tiger's back.

Ono'o shook the monkey off and Juju was thrown into a bush. Mustering up all his strength, Juju aimed one final blow. But then, about a dozen arrows whizzed by and hit the startled tiger. A band of Monkatoni monkeys sliced the weakening tiger's side and killed him. Juju's loyal monkeys had saved him.

After Juju was healed, there was a feast for everyone. Everything had gone the right way. The terror of Jungletonia was no more.

What the Judges Said About
Terror of Jungletonia

"The writer has created a whole world, complete with a social system, political intrigue, and a sense of pervasive danger."

About the Author
Monica Chen

Monica is an 11-year-old sixth grader from California who enjoys swimming and playing the violin. She has traveled with her family to Taiwan, Europe, and South America.

Monica enjoys writing all kinds of stories, especially the "action" parts. If she could be any character in a fantasy story, it would be Meg Murry in *A Wrinkle in Time* because she goes through many exciting and mysterious adventures.

The Match of Freedom ★

By Christina Hansen

Megan Hunnington had lived in an orphanage for as long as she could remember. Days after her 10th birthday, she was adopted by the McJohnsons. They were kind and took her to live with them in the Land Between the Peaks. Megan became friends with Hannah who lived in the cabin next door. Hannah helped Megan understand the mysterious place that was now her home. Megan learned that only people with special powers lived there. The McJohnsons were magical and had sensed that Megan was too. Hannah explained that her gift was invisibility, but Megan had yet to discover her gift.

Megan was happy. There was only one thing everyone feared — the Witch of the Darkness. She was an evil Witch who supposedly only came out at night because the sun's light and heat would cause her to wither away. Hannah had grown up fearful of the Witch, but Megan did not yet understand the danger.

She had been visiting at Hannah's one afternoon, but had stayed too late. It was almost dark when Megan started for home, so Hannah offered to walk Megan halfway since the cabins were far apart. As they stepped out of the light coming through the windows, they heard something crunch in the snow. The Witch of the Darkness appeared. She was wearing sunglasses, which seemed odd on a foggy, February evening.

Hannah was so horrified that she forgot about Megan and became invisible. Megan screamed as the witch grabbed at her. Invisible Hannah pushed the Witch who fell on the ground. Her sunglasses fell off, and Hannah stomped on them. "You'll pay for this!" the Witch howled.

The Witch frantically tried to put the glasses back together. While she was distracted, Hannah remembered the Witch's weaknesses. Thinking quickly, she pulled one long match from her dress pocket. One of Hannah's chores was to light the lanterns each evening. Silently she crept up behind the fidgeting Witch and stuck the burning match into the snow at the hem of the Witch's skirt.

Glancing up, the Witch noticed that Megan was staring at something. Before the Witch could speak, her dress burst into flames and she began to dissolve. This would have been a reason to cheer, but Hannah had been standing too close, and her own dress had also caught on fire. Megan realized she had to do something to help.

She leaped into the air. Although she had never tried it, she somehow knew that she could fly. She soared above the area trying to see the community well. She spied it, landed, and was able to haul a bucket up within seconds. Flying quickly, Megan returned and splashed chilly water on her friend. Hannah's dress sizzled, and the flames went out.

People slowly came out of their cabins. They had been watching in fear, not believing that the Witch of the Darkness had finally been defeated. For so many years, people had lived in fear, but now two young girls had freed them.

What the Judges Said About
The Match of Freedom

"Suspense and humor, irresistible ingredients for a spellbinding story."

About the Author
Christina Hansen

Christina is 10 years old and a fourth grade student in Georgia. She has an older sister named Lauren. Their family has three pets: a horse named Cat, a cat named Stella, and a dog named Buddy. Christina, who has kept a journal since she was in kindergarten, would like to be a writer because it would allow her to be herself and to have fun at the same time. Her favorite part of writing a story is designing the characters who have their own unique names and personalities. Her favorite fantasy author is J.K. Rowling because she keeps her readers in suspense and never gives things away and the ending is always what you don't expect.

The Sea Hag's Riddle

By Zade Henry

I used to think I was beautiful. My name is Grisilda, and I have been cursed to guard this treasure. Part of this curse has turned me into this...creature.

I had long, blonde hair; dark, purple eyes; and a smile that stole the hearts of men. I've been seeking someone who can answer my riddle, and break my curse. If they answer correctly, the treasure is theirs. Answer incorrectly, and I must eat them. Rules are rules, but I never wanted to be a Sea Hag in the first place.

Today, a knight came to win the treasure. He said, "I know what you guard. Hand it over so I may become king."

"You must answer this riddle first. Answer incorrectly, and you are breakfast. Do you agree?"

"Yes."

"What rules the earth with united mind, and spoils the land with men unkind? What makes us love that we should hate, and opens the path to Heaven's Gate?"

"Hmm," he said. "The sword. It can make you king, and force men to obey your command. It can be used for evil or good..."

Knights are pretty tasty once you get them out of the can....

Next, a caravan of wagons came rolling along. One large man stepped out wearing gold and purple robes. "Sea Hag, give me the treasure. I wish to become the wealthiest man on the planet."

I posed the riddle. The merchant said, "Gold. Gold can buy all the land a man can see and brings upon men greed. It can purchase friendship, and pave the streets of heaven."

Once you get past the smell of merchants, they are almost as tasty as knights.

In the evening, a little girl approached my cave, sobbing and wearing tattered clothes. "Little girl," I said, "you come seeking the treasure, correct?"

She said, "I have nothing to lose. My parents and sister have been killed by a disease without a cure. I, too, may be sick. Ask."

I posed the riddle. The girl sobbed, then spoke clearly and directly.

"The heart," she said. "The heart controls us all, and

can make us do good or evil. If we follow our hearts and if we love others first, then we shall receive love in return. Love is the key to Heaven, and love is your answer."

I smiled. "You have answered correctly. Please take your treasure, and remove the curse that has haunted me."

"No, I don't want the treasure," said the girl. "I just need a friend. That's more valuable than any treasure."

I felt the change immediately. The curse had been broken. My hair did not return to its blonde color; my eyes did not turn purple again. There was no change to my skin or smile, but that didn't matter. The only thing that mattered was the change in my heart.

We still guard the cave, she and I, but we guard a friendship that is beyond all treasures and will last forever.

What the Judges Said About
The Sea Hag's Riddle

"Clever and well-written...entertaining and good to read...a clever way to examine the question of what is truly of value — power, wealth, or love."

About the Author
Zade Henry

Zade is 11 years old and likes to read, play games, draw, and practice Tae Kwon Do. She lives in Kansas and is the second oldest child of four children in her family. The other "members" of her family are 16 cats, a dog, and an iguana. Finishing a story is Zade's favorite part of writing. Her favorite fantasy authors are Margaret Weis and Tracy Hickman. If Zade could be any character in a fantasy story, she would be Link from the *Legend of Zelda*.

Dragon Tears

By Kiersten Knoppel

Long ago, but not so very long ago, there lived a motherless girl who was born with an unusual awareness. She had an especially sensitive nose that allowed her to tell what others felt by the particular scent they put out. Violet lived with her father who was elderly and ailing. Because he couldn't work, their cottage was often filled with the aroma of boiled cornhusks and old mushrooms. But that couldn't mask the smell of fear and death in the room. Violet's father was dying, and she despised the fact that she couldn't pinch her nose and make it go away.

Whenever Violet prepared to leave the cottage, her nostrils would fill with the smell of terror. Her father didn't want her to leave. She knew that she needed to summon some help from the village, but it hurt her heart to see her father in such pain, so she stayed close. That night, when she was sleeping, she had an extraordinary dream. Her dead mother appeared to her and advised, "You have the gift of your nose and the power in your heart to save your father. You must go into the city of reason and place the stone that I gave you on the roots of the crooked tree with the spiny leaves." Violet woke up and her loft smelled like love.

When the animals became still and the landscape was shadowed, Violet stood on the threshold of her doorway. A wall of terror blocked the opening. It was her own, and her father's, but the young girl knew what she had to do. Violet blocked her nose, and ran. She followed the scent of fear to the edge of a cliff. A polar bird was there waiting. This creature had the strength of a bear and the swiftness of a bird. It flew her to the city of reason.

In the city of reason, the people's faces were like pictures that never moved. The vacant eyes stared straight ahead, as if in a frozen mask. Despite their best intentions, many emotions leaked out of their pores. The hope, fear, and pain wrapped around her like the mottled skin on an enchanted frog. It showed her where to go.

Shortly, she found herself under the mysterious tree. Violet placed the stone on the ground. The mask people disappeared, forming a tornado of light around her. In their places shot red-orange flames, followed by rough scales that belonged to dragons. As they began to take shape, Violet smelled every dragon. One was timid.

Violet approached the dragon and instinctually began humming, the way a mother would hum to a child. And there, in the corner of the dragon's eye was a tear; the kind of tear one would have if they had known great loneliness. As she leaned over to drink the tear, far away, Violet's father sat up and noticed that the aroma of fear and death was gone.

What the Judges Said About
Dragon Tears

"This is a sensitive and beautifully crafted story. Kiersten's grasp of language is terrific..."

About the Author
Kiersten Knoppel

Kiersten is a nine-year-old fifth grader who lives in California, likes ginger peach tea, and has a dog and a cat. Her older brother is named Tyler. When Kiersten is older she would like to write and be a college professor. Kiersten's mother is a storyteller and she told Kiersten that as soon as she could talk, she was telling stories, too. Kiersten likes to write many different kinds of stories and likes the "aha" moment when a good idea comes. Her favorite author of fantasy stories is Jenny Nimmo.

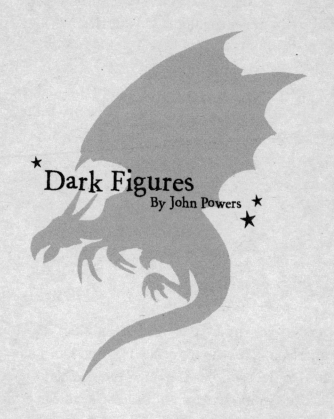

Dark Figures

By John Powers

One cold, lightless night, two strangers in dark coats were seen hastening down Baker Street. One was dressed in a black coat that melted into the darkness. The other had a gray coat that was dull, but shone like the sun when it caught light. The black figure stopped and took from his pocket a gray, rectangular-like device. He then pulled a little box from his other pocket. He inserted it into the top of the device. The screen lit up almost instantly. He looked down for a second and then pointed west. He then proceeded to walk in that direction. The gray one followed. They continued this way until finally they stopped at a door. The black one knocked two times.

"Password," said a grisly voice.

"Anubas," replied the one in black.

The door opened. "Come in," said the deep voice. They entered.

The man who had let them in continued, and said, "Welcome, I am Keystone."

The one in black took off his hood. Dark brown hair and green eyes showed Madarian blood. "I'm Karnar, but call me Mark," he said.

The other figure pulled her hood off and shook her head. Golden hair tumbled out. Her light skin and golden eyes matched. "I'm Eleanor," she said.

"Do you have it?" questioned Mark.

"Yes, I do," replied Keystone. He held out a small black disc. Mark took out a bag filled with gold. They traded. Mark quickly took out a large, round object. He pushed a button and the top rose. He put the disc inside and shut it. Then, he stuck his Portable Map Device on top.

"Finally," Mark impatiently complained. The girl looked on with anticipation. He pushed a button on the PMD and a giant, blue-colored spiral rose in front of them.

"Wow," Eleanor exclaimed. "A real-life portal!"

"Well, this should take us to Madar," Mark commented. He then jumped in. With a flash of blue, he was gone. Eleanor looked around uncertainly and then jumped in. Her atoms instantly dissolved and raced across half the universe.

In a second, she was on the planet Madar. She could see Mark talking with his friend Queso from Valoc. She didn't have any friends here at the Peace Corps of the Universe. She had just been "taken." Queso walked over. "So you must be the new one from Earth. Glad to meet you. Hope the UC didn't scare you—the portal, I mean."

"No, it didn't," she replied.

"Well, it scared me on..." A loud siren interrupted him.

"Oh no, it's the Emergency Siren," sighed Mark.

"What?" questioned Eleanor, but Mark didn't hear her. He hurried off. She followed, but she lost him. She kept turning corners and finally, came to a dead end with one door. Eleanor hesitated, but still entered. As her eyes adjusted to the light, she saw something in a chair.

"Hello," it said. "We've been waiting for you, Miss Chelton."

What the Judges Said About
Dark Figures

"A great opening paragraph. Fun and suspenseful.

About the Author
John Powers

John, who is in seventh grade, makes his home in Florida. He and his family like to go to their condo at the beach. He is one of seven children and his family has 13 pets. He loves reading, would like to write as a career, and his favorite part of story writing is the "planning part." Jenny Nimmo is his favorite fantasy author. If John could be any character in a fantasy story, it would be Gregor from *Gregor the Overlander*.

The Secret of Time

By Bridget R. Wheeler

PROLOGUE

A clock is a device of time to most. But clocks have found their way to being devices of death to some.

A cool wind was blowing through her ragged, curly brown hair. She stood alone on a boulder in the mountains, the tiny golden watch ticking in her hand. Her name was Lani. *Your name is important*, Lani always thought.

So were clocks.

The clock she held had no numbers; but strange symbols of time, like vines, serpents, and black flowers. It was extremely powerful, and could destroy a life if used incorrectly. It had been created by the magic of lightning crashing into the sun.

Lani was a young elf and had spent a good portion of her life searching for this powerful clock. She knew exactly what she was going to do with it. She held the clock up to the sunlight. The arrows stopped moving.

Lani entered her home, a small cave. She was shaken; the symbols weren't exactly what she had expected. She dropped the clock into her robe pocket.

The wizard who taught her magic planted into her mind what the symbol of the snake always meant...

Death.

There were two snake symbols on the clock. If the arrows landed on both of them...Lani shuddered. She wondered hopefully if the clock didn't really work, didn't tell the truth.

Lani left her mountain. She stood in the forest that trimmed the village below. She watched as a band of scruffy men dragged an old cart across a path.

One of them looked up.

"Lads! Look at the lovely little maid! A bit...fancy, isn't she? Probably got some nice trinkets and money in 'er pockets!"

"It'll only take me one shot," said another, hefting his bow. Taking quick aim, he fired.

If Lani hadn't been so surprised, she would have darted away. She practically did...with an arrow in her chest.

She was in the sky upon black clouds, dead...and in pain. She deserved to be there; her evil images of power and destruction were to blame for this! Through the clouds she saw the bandits poking her dead body, rummaging through her pockets. One triumphantly held up the clock.

The destiny of the clock was in the hands of the bandits.

The bandit who had found the clock gazed at it cheerfully. Unfortunately, he slipped on the muddy riverbank and fell. The clock floated away in the river. The man shouted helplessly for it to come back until his companions impatiently pushed him into the river, telling him to find his precious clock. He never did.

The little girl was six when she first went to the river. No one would have guessed she would find the golden object.

When she held it up gleefully, her father rushed it to town where a jeweler bought it for a fine price. He lost it in a storm.

No one knows what happened to the clock, but from a small amount of study, Lani herself up in the sky with an eternal pain in her chest discovered that the arrows always landed on the snakes...and they always told the truth.

What the Judges Said About The Secret of Time

"I love the idea that the main character is obsessed with obtaining this clock thinking somehow she's going to harness the power of time. But that's an illusion, because she's as vulnerable to time as anyone."

About the Author Bridget R. Wheeler

Bridget is 10 years old and is from Vermont. Her family has six children and she is the youngest. Eight cats are also part of the family. Bridget has been writing since she was six years old. Her favorite part of writing a story is inventing new things, creatures, and worlds. She loves the challenges and difficulties of story writing. Her favorite fantasy author is Terry Pratchett. If Bridget could choose a fantasy character as a best friend, hers would be Gonff the Thief (from *Mossflower* and *The Legend of Luke*).

Holly Black
Favorite Fantasy Books Read as a Child:

The most memorable fantasy book Holly read as a child was really a series, The Prydain Chronicles by Lloyd Alexander. "Those books had a huge influence on me. They are probably the books that convinced me that I wanted to be a fantasy writer in the first place."

Suzanne Collins
A Wrinkle in Time by Madeleine L'Engle
The Giver by Lois Lowry
Tuck Everlasting by Natalie Babbitt
The Lord of the Rings by J.R.R. Tolkien
Alice in Wonderland by Lewis Carroll

She says, "The fantasy book that made a real impression on me was *A Wrinkle in Time* by Madeleine L'Engle. I read it in fifth grade and it blew me away. You can see the influence in the first book in my series, Gregor the

Overlander. In that story, Gregor leaves his everyday world and goes on a quest for his father, just as Meg does in *A Wrinkle in Time*. A lot of stories involve a father quest, but Meg's journey was one that really stuck in my mind."

Jenny Nimmo

The Little Prince by Antoine de Saint-Exupery
Frankenstein by Mary Shelley
The Lord of The Rings by J.RR Tolkien
The Lion, the Witch and the Wardrobe by C.S. Lewis
The Changeover by Margaret Mahy

Nimmo says, *The Lion, the Witch and the Wardrobe* by C.S. Lewis was my favorite fantasy when I was nine. The moment when Lucy steps from the real world into Narnia is always at the back of my mind when my very ordinary protagonists gradually (sometimes suddenly) discover that they are extra-ordinary. Perhaps this has influenced my life, in that I am always hopeful."

★ ★ WRITING TIPS FROM OUR JUDGES ★

Jenny Nimmo says, "The best tip I can give is read as many books as you can, and how about trying a good broadsheet (newspaper) now and again. It's surprising what you can find out."

Suzanne Collins says, "Write about things you love. The Underland Chronicles are packed with things I love – animals, kids, sword fighting, fantasy, family. If you fill your stories with things you feel passionately about, it's a whole lot easier for you to write, and a whole lot more exciting for the person reading it."

Holly Black says, "If I could give my younger self some writing tips, the first one would be to read everything. Everything. Literary fiction. Mysteries. Non-fiction. The back of the shampoo bottle. Everything. The second one would be to write a lot. The third would be to find someone equally serious, who can give you an honest opinion about your work and push you to produce more of it."

Some questions to keep in mind when writing fantasy

★ What is the name of your fantasy world? Describe it.

★ What are the first three things you see in your world?

★ What is the name of your hero or heroine? What about your villain?

★ What special powers or abilities do your characters have?

★ What unusual event happens at the start of your story?